The Dreamkeeper's Lantern

Veyndro Weiss

Contents

Chapter 1: The Mystery of the Fading Night

The village of Moonvale slept beneath a sky scattered with silver stars, its cobbled streets bathed in the pale glow of the crescent moon. Yet, despite the peaceful night, Mira lay awake, staring at the wooden beams of her ceiling. She had always been different from the other children—while they awoke each morning with empty minds, their dreams slipping away like mist at sunrise, she could still feel the faint echoes of something missing, something just beyond her reach.

Tonight, however, something was different.

A soft golden glow flickered just outside her window, pulsing like a heartbeat against the darkness. Mira's breath caught. She pushed aside her blanket, careful not to wake her parents, and tiptoed across the wooden floor. Peering out, she saw a tiny, floating light hovering near the ancient willow tree by the river. It wasn't a lantern, nor a firefly—something about it felt… alive.

Heart pounding with curiosity, she pulled on her boots and slipped into the cool night air.

The cobbled streets were empty, the only sound the gentle rustling of wind through the trees. She followed the glow, drawn to it like a moth to a flame, until she reached the willow tree. The golden light hovered just above the ground, illuminating something nestled between the tree's gnarled roots.

A lantern.

But it was unlike any lantern she had ever seen. It was old, its metal frame weathered and adorned with intricate carvings of stars and swirling mist. The glass casing shimmered, holding not a flame, but a swirling golden essence that pulsed gently, as if breathing.

Mira hesitated, then reached out a trembling hand. As soon as her fingers brushed the lantern's surface, a tiny voice, soft as the whispering wind, filled the air.

"You are not meant to be here," it said.

Mira gasped and took a step back. The golden glow pulsed again, and from within the lantern, a small creature emerged—a firefly, yet unlike any she had seen before. Its wings shimmered like liquid gold, its eyes glowed with intelligence.

"I am Flicker," the firefly said. "Keeper of what remains."

Mira's heart pounded in her chest. "What remains of what?"

Flicker hovered closer, his glow illuminating her face. "The dreams," he whispered. "The ones that refuse to be forgotten."

Mira's breath caught. "You mean… the dreams that vanish every morning?"

Flicker bobbed in the air. "Yes. But not all of them vanish completely. Some linger. Some fight to stay. And some—" he paused, his glow dimming slightly, "—are stolen."

Mira's skin prickled. "Stolen?"

Flicker dipped lower, hovering near the lantern. "There is more to your village's curse than you have been told, Mira. And if you wish to uncover the truth, you must be willing to follow the path that lies ahead."

Mira clenched her fists. She had spent her whole life questioning why Moonvale's dreams disappeared, why no one seemed to remember their slumbering adventures. If this tiny firefly held even a fraction of the answer, she wasn't about to turn away.

She took a deep breath and met Flicker's glowing gaze. "Then tell me what I need to do."

Flicker's light flared, casting shadows against the willow tree. "Take the lantern. Protect its light. And find the Library of Lost Dreams before it is too late."

A cold breeze swept through the village, rustling the leaves. Mira reached down and grasped the lantern's handle. The moment she lifted it, the golden glow surged, and for the briefest instant, she felt something stir deep inside her—a forgotten whisper, a half-remembered dream.

And then, just as quickly, it was gone.

She tightened her grip. Whatever lay ahead, she was ready.

The journey had begun.

Chapter 2: The Path of Forgotten Dreams

Mira stood beneath the willow tree, the Dreamkeeper's Lantern clutched in her hands. Its golden glow cast flickering shadows along the cobbled path that led deeper into the village. The weight of its presence filled her with a strange mix of exhilaration and trepidation.

"Where do we start?" she asked Flicker, who hovered beside her, his light pulsing with quiet resolve.

"The map," Flicker said. "You must find it."

Mira frowned. "What map?"

"The one left behind by those who sought the Library before you."

Her pulse quickened. If there was a map, then others had once tried to uncover the truth about the stolen dreams. And yet, no one in Moonvale ever spoke of such things. Had they failed? Had they been made to forget?

She glanced back toward her house, its windows dark and still. If she went inside now, would she be able to find this hidden map? Would her parents wake and stop her?

Determined, she hurried through the quiet streets, the lantern's glow her only guide. The village was eerily silent, as if the very air held its breath. When she reached her home, she hesitated, then slipped through the door.

Inside, the house was steeped in shadows. The floorboards creaked beneath her careful steps as she made her way to the small attic storage above her room. If a map existed, it had to be there—among the forgotten relics of her family's past.

She pushed open the attic door, dust swirling in the air. Moonlight filtered through the small window, illuminating rows of old trunks and faded books. She knelt beside the largest trunk and lifted the lid. Inside, bundled beneath a worn quilt, was an old leather-bound journal.

She opened it carefully, her fingers brushing against brittle pages filled with delicate handwriting. Near the center of the book, something unusual caught her eye—a folded parchment tucked between the pages. Mira pulled it free and carefully unfolded it.

Her breath hitched. It was a map.

Lines of ink wove a winding path from Moonvale to the unknown. At the farthest edge of the parchment, just beyond the Whispershade Woods, was a symbol: a book surrounded by stars. The Library of Lost Dreams.

Mira's fingers trembled as she traced the path. "It's real," she whispered.

Flicker landed on her shoulder, his light reflecting off the ink. "Then there is still hope."

A creak from downstairs made Mira freeze. Her parents were stirring.

She folded the map, tucked it into her satchel, and grabbed the lantern. She had no time to waste.

With one last glance at the house that had always been her home, she turned and stepped into the night, the path ahead uncertain, but her heart set on finding the truth.

The journey had truly begun.

Chapter 3: The Whispershade Woods

Mira tightened her grip on the lantern as she stepped beyond the village's outskirts. The cobbled streets gave way to a narrow dirt path, winding toward the looming silhouette of the Whispershade Woods. The trees there stood like silent sentinels, their gnarled branches twisting toward the sky. A cold wind stirred the leaves, carrying with it a hushed murmur—almost as if the forest itself was whispering.

Flicker flitted beside her, his golden glow cutting through the creeping mist. "Be careful," he warned. "The woods remember every step taken within them. If you do not tread wisely, you may forget why you entered at all."

Mira shivered. "You mean it can make me forget?"

Flicker bobbed solemnly. "Yes. The deeper you go, the heavier the fog becomes. Memories unravel here, like threads from an old tapestry."

Mira exhaled, steadying herself. She had come too far to turn back now. With a determined step, she crossed into the woods.

The air was thick, damp with the scent of moss and earth. Twisted roots snaked across the ground, and the trees loomed closer together, their dark trunks creating an eerie tunnel. Shadows stretched unnaturally, shifting as if watching her. The lantern's glow flickered, casting golden ripples against the mist.

With each step, Mira felt something tug at the edges of her mind. At first, it was subtle—a stray thought slipping from her grasp. Then, as the fog thickened, it became stronger. She paused, struggling to recall where she had been moments ago. Had she already passed that crooked oak? Had the path always twisted in this direction?

Panic fluttered in her chest. Stay focused. She clutched the lantern tighter and tried to recall her purpose. The map. The Library of Lost Dreams. The stolen dreams of Moonvale.

A whisper brushed against her ear. "Mira… turn back… it's too late…"

She spun, heart hammering. The mist swirled, forming shifting figures just beyond sight—flickering silhouettes with hollow eyes. She swallowed hard. Illusions. They can't hurt me.

Flicker's glow flared brighter. "Do not listen to them. Keep moving."

Mira forced herself forward, step by step. But the whispers grew louder, each voice tugging at the corners of her thoughts.

"You don't belong here."

"You will be lost forever."

"They will never remember you."

A cold dread seeped into her bones. What if they were right? What if her parents woke to find her gone and simply… forgot her? What if she vanished from Moonvale's memory just as the dreams had?

She stumbled, knees hitting damp earth. The whispering figures crept closer. The fog thickened, coiling around her like a living thing.

Then, Flicker zipped to her face, his tiny body blazing with golden light. "Mira! The lantern—use it!"

Her breath hitched. She lifted the Dreamkeeper's Lantern, its glow barely visible through the fog. With a shaking hand, she focused on its warmth, on the light still pulsing within.

She closed her eyes. This light is real. I am real. My journey is real.

As if in response to her resolve, the lantern flared. A golden pulse surged outward, tearing through the mist like a dawn breaking over the horizon. The whispering figures recoiled, their forms unraveling like smoke caught in the wind.

The path ahead cleared, and for the first time since entering the forest, Mira could see her way forward.

She pushed herself to her feet. The whispers had faded, but she knew the danger wasn't over. Taking a steadying breath, she tightened her grip on the lantern and stepped deeper into the woods, where the true test awaited her.

The journey was only just beginning.

Chapter 4: The Keeper of Secrets

Mira emerged from the Whispershade Woods just as the first light of dawn painted the horizon in hues of violet and gold. The oppressive fog had thinned, giving way to rolling meadows bathed in morning dew. She inhaled deeply, relief flooding her as the whispers of the forest finally faded behind her.

Before her stood a towering structure of ivy-clad stone—a library unlike any she had ever seen. Its vast walls were adorned with glowing runes, its towering spires vanishing into the clouds. Books drifted through the air, carried by invisible currents, their pages fluttering as though whispering secrets to one another.

Flicker hovered beside her. "The Library of Lost Dreams."

Mira's heart pounded. This was it. The place whispered about in legends, the place that held the lost dreams of Moonvale. She stepped forward, pushing open the massive wooden doors. They creaked, unveiling a grand hall where countless books floated, their words glowing faintly in the dim light.

At the center of the hall stood a peculiar figure—a tall, thin man with silver spectacles perched on the edge of his nose. His cloak shimmered like stardust, and his sharp eyes twinkled with quiet amusement as he observed Mira.

"Ah," he said, closing the book he had been reading. "I was wondering when you would arrive."

Mira hesitated. "You… know me?"

The man smiled. "I know all who seek forgotten things. I am Mr. Thistle, Keeper of the Library. And you, Mira, are here to restore what was lost."

She swallowed. "Then you know about the stolen dreams?"

Mr. Thistle nodded solemnly. "Moonvale's people entrusted their hopes and aspirations to the stars, but over time, belief in magic waned, and the dreams began to fade.

What you see here are the remnants of those forgotten wishes, trapped in these pages." He gestured toward the floating books. "Without someone to remember them, they will be lost forever."

Mira clutched the lantern. "Then I want to help."

Thistle studied her for a long moment, then nodded. "Very well. But retrieving lost dreams is no simple task." He gestured, and a book drifted toward them, its cover glowing faintly. "You must listen to the voices within, find the hearts they belong to, and return them."

Mira hesitated, then reached out. As soon as her fingers touched the cover, the world around her shimmered.

She barely had time to gasp before she was pulled inside the dream.

Chapter 5: Into the Dreamscape

The moment Mira's fingers touched the book's cover, a rush of golden light enveloped her. The library faded, replaced by a swirling expanse of colors—a sky painted in hues of deep indigo, streaked with ribbons of violet and silver. She felt weightless, drifting through the space between waking and dreaming.

Then, with a sudden pull, she landed on solid ground.

Mira gasped. She stood in the middle of a vast city unlike anything she had ever seen. Towering spires of crystal rose into the sky, their surfaces reflecting shifting images of people's deepest desires and forgotten hopes. The streets were paved with luminous stones that pulsed with every step she took. Above, constellations realigned with every breath, forming unfamiliar patterns.

Flicker hovered at her side, his light subdued in the dream's glow. "Welcome to the Dreamscape."

Mira turned in wonder. "This… this is a lost dream?"

Flicker nodded. "Every book in the library holds an entire world within it—a dream once cherished but now abandoned."

Before Mira could respond, a soft melody drifted through the air, haunting and bittersweet. She followed the sound, her heart quickening as she rounded a corner. There, sitting on the edge of a floating bridge, was a young boy dressed in faded clothes. He plucked at the strings of a translucent harp, his expression distant and sorrowful.

Mira stepped closer. "Hello?"

The boy lifted his gaze, his silver eyes flickering with recognition. "You're real?" His voice was barely above a whisper, as though he hadn't spoken in a long time.

She nodded. "I think so."

The boy exhaled, his shoulders slumping. "Then… you shouldn't be here. Dreams don't welcome the waking."

Mira hesitated. "But this is your dream, isn't it?"

The boy flinched. His fingers stilled on the harp strings. "It was," he murmured. "A long time ago."

Flicker drifted closer, his glow intensifying. "Mira, this is the one we were searching for. His dream was lost, but he is still here."

Mira's mind spun. If the dreamer was trapped within his own lost dream, what did that mean for the others? Could there be more like him—people who had vanished from Moonvale, forgotten even by their own families?

She took a steadying breath. "I came here to help," she said. "Will you let me?"

The boy studied her for a long moment, then slowly nodded. "If you can remember me," he whispered, "then maybe I'm not truly lost."

A new resolve bloomed within Mira's chest. She wasn't just retrieving lost dreams—she was bringing back the people who had been forgotten within them.

And she had only just begun.

Chapter 6: The Broken Thread

Mira sat beside the boy on the floating bridge, watching the luminous city shimmer around them. Despite its beauty, an unsettling stillness hung in the air, as if the dream had been abandoned mid-thought.

"What's your name?" she asked gently.

The boy hesitated before answering. "Elias."

Mira offered a small smile. "Elias, I think your dream is calling you back."

Elias lowered his gaze. "It's too late. The thread is broken."

Flicker hovered between them, his glow dim. "The thread?"

Elias nodded toward the sky, where the shifting constellations pulsed with a strange, fading light. "Every dream is connected to the dreamer by an invisible thread. If the thread frays, the dream dims. If it breaks…" His voice trailed off, his silver eyes filled with sorrow. "The dream is lost forever."

Mira's grip tightened around the lantern. "Then we have to fix it."

Elias shook his head. "I've tried. Every time I reach for it, it slips away."

Mira followed his gaze upward. The constellations shimmered, their patterns flickering in and out of focus. If Elias was right, his connection to his dream was unraveling—and if it vanished completely, he might disappear with it.

A cold realization settled over her. How many others had already faded away?

She stood, determination hardening in her chest. "There has to be a way to mend the thread. If we can find where it broke, maybe we can weave it back together."

Elias looked up at her, something like hope flickering in his eyes. "But how?"

Flicker zipped around them, his glow growing stronger. "The Library holds the key. Every lost dream is recorded there. If we find Elias's story, we may find the missing thread."

Mira held out her hand. "Then let's go."

Elias hesitated, then reached for her. The moment their hands touched, the Dreamscape trembled. The stars above realigned, and a golden thread shimmered into existence—thin, frayed, but still holding on.

Mira met Elias's gaze. "We're not too late."

With the lantern's glow lighting their path, they stepped forward together, back toward the Library of Lost Dreams, where the past waited to be rewritten.

Chapter 7: The Forgotten Story

Mira and Elias stepped through the glowing doorway of the Library of Lost Dreams, their hands still clasped as the golden thread between them flickered like a fragile ember. The vast hall stretched endlessly before them, its floating books drifting like quiet ghosts, each holding the remnants of a forgotten dream.

Towering shelves spiraled into infinity, the air thick with the scent of old parchment and the hush of whispered memories. The lantern's glow illuminated the vast space, casting long shadows that flickered like the echoes of lost voices.

Mr. Thistle awaited them at the center of the room, adjusting his silver spectacles as he took in Elias's presence. His expression softened. "Ah. A lost dreamer."

Elias lowered his gaze. "I don't remember how I got here."

Thistle nodded solemnly. "Then we must find your story before it fades completely." He turned, gesturing to the great spirals of bookshelves. "Every dream once held in Moonvale is recorded here, but a lost story is like a missing star—it does not wish to be found."

Mira tightened her grip on the lantern. "Then we'll search until we do."

Thistle studied her for a moment before giving a small nod. With a wave of his hand, books began to glide through the air, their pages fluttering open, revealing glimpses of dreamscapes—children soaring through endless skies, forgotten melodies waiting to be played, unfinished stories longing for an ending.

Some books murmured as they passed, their words barely audible, like echoes of dreams struggling to be heard. Others remained silent, their pages dim, as if the memory they carried had nearly faded from existence.

Elias watched, his silver eyes wide with something between awe and fear. "What if my story isn't here?"

Thistle sighed, his voice tinged with sorrow. "If a dream is truly forgotten, it fades into the void. If that happens, not even the Library can bring it back."

A chill crept down Mira's spine. "Then we have to find it before that happens."

A sudden gust of wind stirred the books around them, causing a flurry of pages to scatter through the air. Then, as if drawn by an unseen force, one book—a small, unassuming volume—tumbled from the shelves and landed at Elias's feet. The cover bore no title, its edges frayed with age. A thin, silvery mist curled around it, shifting and dissolving like the last traces of a forgotten dream.

Elias hesitated, staring at the book as if it might disappear if he moved too quickly. Mira knelt beside him, placing a reassuring hand on his arm.

"This is it," she whispered.

Elias reached for the book, his fingers trembling as he lifted the fragile volume. He turned it over in his hands before opening it—only to find that the pages were blank.

Flicker hovered above them, his glow dimming. "The story is vanishing."

Elias's throat tightened. "Then how do we read it?"

Mira took a deep breath, her heartbeat steadying. "We remember."

She placed her hand on the empty pages, closing her eyes. Slowly, words began to form—faint, like ink bleeding through old parchment. A name appeared first: Elias Vale.

Elias inhaled sharply. "That's me."

Then, as if responding to his voice, the story began to write itself once more. Lines of ink emerged, curling into paragraphs, revealing a past long buried in the depths of the forgotten.

Mira and Elias watched as the pages filled with flickering images—snapshots of another time, another life. A boy standing at the edge of Moonvale's river, his fingers clutching a tattered book. A house with a single candle burning in the window. A sky filled with falling stars, and a wish whispered into the wind.

As the ink settled, the words grew clearer, drawing Elias into a past he could no longer recall.

And with it, the truth of why Elias had been lost.

Chapter 8: The Truth of Elias Vale

As the ink settled upon the pages, Elias stared at the unfolding story, his pulse quickening. Words danced across the parchment, revealing glimpses of a life he could not remember. Mira and Mr. Thistle stood beside him, watching as the lost past came to life.

Elias Vale had once been a boy of Moonvale—a dreamer like Mira, filled with wonder and curiosity. But unlike Mira, Elias had vanished from the town long ago. No one in Moonvale remembered him, as if he had been plucked from existence. His name, his dreams, his very presence had faded like a forgotten whisper.

"How is this possible?" Elias murmured, tracing a trembling finger along the inked lines.

Mr. Thistle sighed, adjusting his spectacles. "There are many ways a dream can be lost. Some are forgotten, some are stolen... and some are willingly given away."

Mira turned to Elias. "Did you give yours away?"

Elias shook his head, frustration clouding his silver eyes. "I don't remember. I don't remember anything before waking up here."

The book's pages turned by themselves, revealing more of his past. There he was, a younger version of himself, standing in the Moonvale fields beneath a sky brimming with stars. He clutched a small, worn notebook close to his chest, scribbling furiously as if afraid the words might escape him.

"He wrote stories," Mira whispered, watching the memory unfold.

Flicker's glow pulsed with recognition. "Not just stories. Dreams."

Elias had not only dreamt like the other children of Moonvale—he had written dreams down, weaving them into words so they would never be forgotten. But something had happened. A shadowy figure loomed at the edge of the memory, barely visible through the pages of the book.

Elias shuddered. "Who is that?"

Mr. Thistle's face darkened. "The one who preys on forgotten things. The Hollow Scribe."

Mira felt a chill creep through her bones. "The Hollow Scribe?"

Thistle nodded gravely. "There are creatures that feed on lost dreams. The Hollow Scribe is the worst of them. It does not merely steal—it consumes. It takes dreams, memories, and even people, leaving only empty spaces where they once existed."

The book revealed the moment Elias had disappeared. The shadow had reached out for him, fingers curling like ink tendrils. Elias, clutching his notebook, had resisted. But the Hollow Scribe was stronger. In an instant, Elias had been erased—his stories, his name, his entire existence swallowed into the void.

Elias's breath hitched. "That's why no one remembers me. Why I don't remember myself."

Mira tightened her grip on his hand. "Then we have to get your story back."

Mr. Thistle gave a slow nod. "Yes. But to do that, you must face the Hollow Scribe. And no one who has gone after it has ever returned."

Chapter 9: The Path to the Hollow Scribe

The library trembled as if it had heard their decision. The books around them fluttered, their pages rustling like voices whispering warnings. Mira swallowed hard, squeezing Elias's hand.

Mr. Thistle adjusted his spectacles, his expression unreadable. "If you seek the Hollow Scribe, you must tread carefully. It dwells in the deepest part of the void, where forgotten things vanish entirely."

Flicker hovered above them, his golden light dimming. "The path is dangerous, but the lantern will guide you—if you are willing to step beyond the known world."

Elias straightened his shoulders. "I want to remember. I want my story back. I can't stay in the shadows any longer."

Mira met his gaze, determination burning in her chest. "Then we'll go together."

Mr. Thistle sighed, then extended his hands, revealing a faded, fragile map. "This will take you to the edge of the Library, to the place where stories dissolve. That is where the Hollow Scribe lingers. But be warned—the void has no mercy for those who hesitate."

Mira accepted the map, the paper cool beneath her fingertips. The ink shifted as if alive, forming a winding path that led into darkness. The very air around the map seemed heavier, as if it knew the weight of the journey ahead. She glanced at Elias. "Are you ready?"

Elias nodded. "I have to be."

A gust of wind swept through the library, rattling the shelves. The books trembled more violently, and several toppled to the floor, their pages flying open. Mira gasped as ink bled off the pages, dissolving into the air like smoke. The Library itself was warning them—this was not a journey one returned from unchanged.

Mr. Thistle's hand twitched as if he wanted to stop them, but he only whispered, "Step forward, and do not look back. Or you may find yourself lost forever."

With a deep breath, Mira tightened her grip on the lantern, and together, she and Elias crossed the threshold—into the heart of the forgotten.

As soon as they stepped forward, the world behind them vanished. The Library of Lost Dreams was gone. They stood on what felt like solid ground, yet when Mira looked down, there was nothing beneath her feet but swirling blackness, stretching infinitely in all directions.

The Void was neither hot nor cold, neither silent nor loud. It was an absence of everything—sound, color, time. It wrapped around them like an unseen presence, pressing against their skin. Flicker's glow flickered unsteadily, his light struggling against the oppressive darkness.

Mira turned to Elias. His face was paler than before, his eyes searching the void. "Do you feel that?" he whispered.

Mira nodded. It was as if the darkness was watching them.

Then, from the depths of the void, a voice slithered toward them. A whisper, just on the edge of hearing.

"You do not belong here."

Chapter 10: The Abyss of Lost Dreams

The whisper coiled around them like an invisible thread, tugging at the edges of their minds. Mira shuddered, gripping the lantern tighter. Flicker's glow flickered dangerously, barely pushing back the overwhelming darkness.

Elias stiffened. "Did you hear that?"

Mira swallowed hard. "I think it heard us first."

The void was no longer silent. Beneath their feet—or the space where ground should have been—shadows writhed like ink spilled across water. The whisper returned, stronger this time, slithering through the abyss.

"Turn back... You do not belong..."

A chilling sensation seeped into Mira's skin, like invisible fingers brushing against her arms. Elias shuddered beside her, clenching his fists.

"No. I won't turn back."

Ahead, the darkness swirled, parting like storm clouds to reveal something massive. An archway loomed before them, ancient and crumbling, carved with symbols Mira couldn't understand. Beyond it stretched an endless corridor, lined with towering shelves that seemed to be made of the same swirling darkness as the void itself. Some shelves twisted unnaturally, spiraling in ways that made Mira's head ache just looking at them.

Mira stepped forward cautiously, running her fingers over the archway's surface. It was colder than ice, yet it pulsed like a living thing beneath her touch. When she withdrew her hand, her fingertips were coated in something dark—like ink that refused to dry.

Flicker dimmed further. "We are in its domain now."

A windless current pulled them forward as they stepped beneath the arch. The corridor stretched endlessly, but Mira knew they were being guided—whether by fate or something more sinister. The lantern pulsed weakly in her hands, as if struggling to stay alight. Shadows slithered between the shelves, darting just beyond the edge of her vision.

"What is this place?" Elias whispered.

"The Abyss of Lost Dreams," Flicker murmured. "Where all forgotten things come to rest."

Elias hesitated. "Then that means my past..."

Mira nodded. "It's here. Somewhere. And so is the Hollow Scribe."

The whispering voices grew louder, shifting into a chorus of murmurs. Words brushed against their ears, fragments of memories, unfinished stories, lost ambitions. Mira heard a child's voice begging to remember a dream of flying. A poet whispering verses that had never been written. A musician playing a song the world had never heard.

Elias flinched. "I hear them too. They're... they're people's dreams, aren't they?"

"Yes," Flicker confirmed. "Trapped."

A gust of cold air swept through the corridor, and the voices stopped. Silence fell, heavy and expectant.

Then, from the depths of the abyss, a new voice emerged. This one was not a whisper. It was low, hollow, and ancient.

"Who dares disturb the realm of the forgotten?"

The darkness ahead shifted. Two pinpricks of tglowing silver light appeared in the void—cycs. But they did not stay still. They blinked, split, multiplied, scattering across the abyss before reforming into a new shape. A towering figure, cloaked in swirling ink-like shadows, stepped forward, its movements fluid yet unnatural. Its body did not hold a single form; one moment it was draped in flowing robes, the next it was skeletal, then formless mist. It was as if it could not decide what it had once been.

Elias sucked in a breath. "Is that... the Hollow Scribe?"

The air around them trembled. The lantern flickered, nearly going out.

"You have come seeking what is lost," the voice continued, dripping with something deeper than malice. "But some things are meant to be forgotten."

Chapter 11: The Hollow Scribe's Bargain

The Hollow Scribe loomed before them, its form constantly shifting—sometimes a hooded figure, sometimes a tangle of ink-like tendrils, sometimes a hollow shell filled with nothing but darkness. Its many eyes gleamed silver, watching Mira and Elias with an eerie stillness.

Mira's fingers tightened around the lantern. It pulsed weakly, its light struggling against the suffocating abyss. Flicker's glow barely illuminated the space around them, casting long, wavering shadows.

"You have come seeking what is lost," the Hollow Scribe intoned, its voice layered with echoes of countless forgotten voices. "But tell me, travelers—what would you offer in return?"

Elias stepped forward before Mira could stop him. His fists were clenched, his jaw tight. "You stole my past. I want it back."

The Scribe tilted its shifting head. "Stole? No, boy. The world forgets, and I simply keep what is abandoned."

Mira swallowed hard. "And if something is taken unfairly? If someone was made to forget?"

The Hollow Scribe's presence darkened, the surrounding shelves trembling as if caught in an invisible wind. The whispers of lost dreams stirred, curling around them like unseen fingers. "Memories, dreams, hopes… they are not so different. They slip through the cracks of time. Some things are meant to be lost."

"No," Elias said, voice unwavering. "Not this time."

A moment of silence stretched between them, tense and unbroken. Then the Hollow Scribe let out something between a chuckle and a sigh—a hollow, rattling sound.

"There is always a price," it said at last. "If you wish to reclaim what is lost, then something must be given in exchange."

Mira's stomach twisted. She knew this moment would come. Magic like this—ancient, powerful—was never free. She thought of Elias, of the pain in his eyes, the questions that had haunted him all his life. Could they walk away now?

"What kind of price?" she asked carefully.

The Hollow Scribe's form twisted, its tendrils unfurling like ink dissolving in water. It gestured toward the abyss beyond the shelves. "A trade. A memory for a memory. A dream for a dream. One of you must give up something precious—something you would never wish to forget."

Mira's breath caught in her throat.

Elias looked at her, his expression unreadable. Then he turned back to the Hollow Scribe. "If I do this… if I give you something important… will you return my past?"

The Hollow Scribe's shifting form stilled. "Yes."

Flicker's glow dimmed further. "Mira," the little light whispered urgently. "Be careful. There are memories that, once given, can never be reclaimed."

Mira's mind raced. If Elias gave up something—what would happen to him? Would it change who he was? Would he even be the same person when they left this place?

She turned to him, heart pounding. "Elias… don't rush this."

But Elias took a deep breath, eyes locked onto the Hollow Scribe.

"I'll do it."

The Hollow Scribe's many eyes gleamed with something unreadable. "Then step forward, and let the trade begin."

Chapter 12: The Memory Exchange

The air in the abyss thickened as Elias stepped forward. Mira wanted to grab his arm, to stop him before it was too late—but something held her in place. It wasn't fear. It was the gravity of the moment, the unshakable knowledge that what was about to happen could not be undone.

The Hollow Scribe stretched out a shifting limb, its tendrils coiling into something that almost resembled fingers. "Close your eyes, child of the forgotten. Speak the memory you wish to surrender."

Elias hesitated. His breath came quick and shallow. Mira could see the battle raging inside him—what to give, what to keep.

Then, finally, he spoke. "I… I give the memory of my mother's voice."

Mira's heart clenched. A piece of Elias—one of the only things he had left, a fragment of warmth in his uncertain past—he was about to let it go.

The Hollow Scribe's many eyes shimmered, its form shifting once more. "Accepted."

A gust of invisible force swept through the abyss, coiling around Elias like a phantom wind. His eyes widened in shock as a flickering golden thread unraveled from his temple, stretching toward the Hollow Scribe's waiting grasp. The moment it touched the entity's fingers, the thread dissolved into the swirling darkness.

Elias staggered, his hand flying to his head as if trying to hold onto something slipping away. His face twisted in confusion.

"What… what was I saying?"

Mira sucked in a breath. He didn't even remember what he had given up.

The Hollow Scribe straightened, the abyss itself seeming to pulse in response. "The trade is complete. Now, take what you came for."

From within the shadows, something took form. A small, silver orb emerged, pulsating like a heartbeat. It floated toward Elias, hovering just before his chest. Mira held her breath as he reached out, his fingers trembling.

The moment he touched it, the orb burst into a cascade of light. Images flooded Elias's mind—memories snapping back into place like a long-lost puzzle. He gasped, stumbling backward as the weight of it all crashed down on him.

Mira caught him before he fell. "Elias! What do you see?"

He squeezed his eyes shut, clutching his head. "I… I remember. My home. My father. The night I was taken…"

A shudder ran through him as he exhaled, looking up at her with wide, almost disbelieving eyes. "Mira… I had a sister."

Mira blinked. "You—what?"

But before he could say more, the Hollow Scribe's voice slithered through the air once more. "You have taken what you sought. Now go."

The shadows around them began to shift, the abyss closing in. The towering shelves of forgotten dreams creaked as if the world itself was exhaling. The Hollow Scribe turned, its form dissolving back into the endless dark.

Flicker's glow brightened. "We have to move!"

Mira grabbed Elias's hand and ran. The abyss trembled behind them, the whispers growing louder, reaching for them with unseen hands. But as they passed beneath the archway they had entered through, the darkness broke apart—dissipating into nothingness like a dream at dawn.

They stumbled into the dim light of reality, breathless, shaken, and forever changed.

Chapter 13: Echoes of the Forgotten

The night air was cold as Mira and Elias stumbled away from the Hollow Scribe's domain. The shadows of the forgotten realm still clung to them, whispering at the edges of their minds. The lantern in Mira's grip flickered weakly, its once-steady glow faltering. Even Flicker, usually a warm beacon, seemed dimmer.

Elias clutched his head, his breath uneven. "I had a sister…" he whispered again, as if saying the words aloud would make them more real. "But why don't I remember her name? Why don't I remember her face?"

Mira swallowed hard. She knew what the Hollow Scribe had taken from him—the sound of his mother's voice. Without it, the memories that had returned were fractured, incomplete.

"Maybe… maybe the answers are still out there," she said, placing a hand on his arm. "We just have to find them."

Elias exhaled shakily. "I need to know what happened to her. If she's still out there…"

Flicker darted closer, its dim glow pulsing anxiously. "If she was taken, there's only one place left to search. The place where the truly forgotten dwell."

Mira and Elias exchanged glances. "You mean—?"

Flicker hesitated, then whispered, "The Lost Veil."

A chill ran down Mira's spine. She had heard stories—old, half-remembered tales of a place where abandoned dreams and vanished souls drifted, unseen and unreachable. A place where even time itself unraveled.

Elias straightened. There was something new in his expression—determination, edged with something deeper. "Then that's where we're going."

Mira nodded. "We'll find her, Elias. No matter what."

Above them, the sky stretched vast and endless, the stars watching silently. And somewhere beyond the veil of memory and time, the answers waited—waiting to be reclaimed.

They trekked through the moonlit valley, following Flicker's faint glow. The path ahead was uncertain, the air thick with the weight of unanswered questions. As they walked, Elias kept his hands clenched into fists at his sides, his jaw tight.

"What if she's forgotten me?" he muttered. "What if... I find her, and she doesn't even know who I am?"

Mira considered his words carefully. "Then we remind her," she said softly. "Just like we reminded the villagers of their dreams. Just like we reminded you."

Elias let out a shaky breath. "I just... I don't know if I can go through losing her again."

Mira hesitated before reaching for his hand, giving it a firm squeeze. "You won't be alone. We'll do this together."

They walked in silence for a while, the only sounds their footsteps against the damp earth and the occasional rustling of unseen creatures in the underbrush. The landscape around them was shifting—familiar trees becoming gnarled, their trunks twisting in ways that defied nature. The ground sloped downward, guiding them toward something unseen. It felt like the world itself was nudging them forward, whispering their fate in the wind.

Flicker pulsed ahead of them, leading the way. "We're close now," it murmured. "The entrance to the Lost Veil is near."

Mira exchanged a glance with Elias. Whatever lay ahead, there was no turning back now.

Chapter 14: The Threshold of the Lost Veil

The path ahead twisted into the unknown, and with every step, Mira felt a weight pressing down on her. The world around them had begun to change—colors dulled, sounds became distant, and even the air carried an eerie stillness. It was as if they had wandered into the space between waking and dreaming.

"We're close," Flicker whispered, its glow flickering uneasily. "The boundary between this world and the Lost Veil is thin here."

Elias tightened his grip on the Dreamkeeper's Lantern, his knuckles white. "What exactly are we walking into?"

Flicker hesitated before answering. "A place where time forgets and where memories drift without anchors. Those who remain there are neither lost nor found. They simply... linger."

A shiver ran down Mira's spine. She had always believed that dreams, even the forgotten ones, still carried echoes in the world. But the idea of people becoming trapped—lost within the remnants of something unfinished—unnerved her.

Ahead, the trees bent unnaturally, forming an archway of interwoven branches. A dense mist clung to the ground, swirling in unseen currents. It reminded Mira of the way dreams dissolved upon waking—unpredictable, fleeting.

"This is the entrance," Flicker said. "Once we step through, there may be no clear way back."

Elias took a deep breath. "Then we step through together."

Mira nodded, her heart pounding. She had come this far. There was no turning back now.

With a final glance at each other, they stepped into the mist, leaving the world they knew behind.

The moment they crossed the threshold, a strange sensation washed over them. The mist thickened, muffling all sound except for the rhythmic thudding of their own hearts. The trees around them seemed to shift, stretching impossibly high, their bark dark and cracked like forgotten pages in an ancient book.

Mira gasped as her vision blurred for a moment. Images flashed through her mind—faces she didn't recognize, voices calling names that weren't hers. The sensation passed as quickly as it came, leaving her breathless.

"Did you feel that?" she asked, gripping Elias's arm.

He gave a slow nod, his expression distant. "It's like… memories that don't belong to me."

Flicker fluttered beside them, its glow dim but steady. "The Lost Veil does not simply take people. It takes their stories, weaving them into the fabric of its existence. Be careful. Not all memories here will be yours."

A cold wind whispered through the trees, carrying fragments of voices—some pleading, some laughing, others nothing more than a sigh lost in time. Mira clenched her fists. Somewhere in this eerie, shifting world, Elias's sister was waiting. And they would find her, no matter what it took.

Chapter 15: Whispers of the Lost

The mist swallowed them whole, its silvery tendrils coiling around Mira, Elias, and Flicker as they moved forward. The world beyond the threshold was unlike anything Mira had ever seen. Shadows wavered like forgotten echoes, and the very air shimmered as if it held remnants of half-remembered dreams. Time felt different here—stretched, tangled, and uncertain.

"Stay close," Flicker murmured, its glow dimming under the weight of the Veil's presence. "This place feeds on the forgotten. If you stray too far, you may not find your way back."

Elias inhaled sharply, his fingers clenching the Dreamkeeper's Lantern. "Do you hear that?"

Mira stilled. At first, there was only silence. Then, a whisper—faint, barely more than a breath of wind. It curled around them, threading through the mist, an indistinct murmur of voices layered over one another.

"Elias…"

The voice was fragile, like a ripple across still water.
Elias stiffened. "That's her." He turned, scanning the haze,
his expression frantic. "I heard her!"

Mira grabbed his wrist before he could take a step.
"Elias, wait! We don't know what's out there."

His jaw tightened, but he nodded, forcing himself to stay
still.

Flicker flitted ahead, leading them through the shifting
landscape. Structures loomed in the mist—half-formed
towers that seemed to melt into the sky, staircases that led
to nowhere, doors standing alone with no walls to hold
them. The Lost Veil was a realm of forgotten places as well
as forgotten people.

As they moved deeper, the whispers grew stronger, no
longer just echoes but discernible words.

"Who… are you?"

Mira's heart pounded. The voice was close now.

Elias swallowed hard, stepping forward. "Lena?" he called into the mist. "Is that you?"

For a moment, silence. Then, a figure emerged—a girl no older than fifteen, her form flickering at the edges, like an image reflected in a rippling pond. Her eyes, wide with recognition, met Elias's.

"Elias?" she whispered.

His breath hitched. "Lena. I found you."

But before he could step closer, the mist surged between them, and the shadows stirred.

Chapter 16: Shadows Between Worlds

Elias lunged forward, but the mist thickened, swirling like a living thing, wrapping around Lena and obscuring her form. His voice cracked as he shouted, "Lena! Hold on!"

The girl's image wavered, her lips moving without sound, her eyes desperate. Then, the mist pulled her back, her figure dissolving into the shifting haze.

"No!" Elias swung the lantern toward the mist, its golden glow barely piercing the dense fog. "Where did she go?"

Mira reached for him, gripping his arm to steady him. "She's still here. We just have to find a way to reach her."

Flicker zipped in frantic circles, its glow flickering like a candle in the wind. "The Veil doesn't just separate the lost—it weaves them into itself. If we don't act quickly, she'll be absorbed into the dreamscape entirely."

Elias turned to Flicker, his eyes burning with determination. "How do we stop that?"

Flicker hesitated before whispering, "We must find the Anchor. Every trapped soul here is bound to a memory—an anchor that ties them to this place. If we can uncover Lena's, we might be able to pull her free."

Mira nodded. "Then we start looking."

The three of them pressed forward through the shifting fog. Strange shapes loomed in the distance—distorted remnants of forgotten places. A crumbling bridge stretched halfway across nothingness. A shattered clock tower hung suspended in the mist, its hands frozen at midnight. And along the ground, barely visible through the haze, were scattered remnants of lost dreams—faded books, broken toys, torn photographs.

Mira knelt beside a doll with missing button eyes, running her fingers over its worn fabric. "Do all these belong to people who were lost?"

Flicker hovered close. "Yes. Fragments of what once mattered."

Elias's fists clenched. "Then Lena's anchor must be here somewhere."

They pressed on, deeper into the Veil, searching through the echoes of forgotten lives. But with each passing moment, the mist grew colder, the shadows darker, and the whispers louder.

They weren't alone.

Something else was watching them.

Chapter 17: The Anchor of Memory

The mist thickened as Mira, Elias, and Flicker pushed forward, their breath coming in short bursts. Every step felt heavier, as if the Veil itself resisted their passage. The scattered fragments of forgotten lives surrounded them—echoes of laughter, whispers of sorrow, and shadows of dreams lost to time.

Elias scanned the shifting landscape, his grip tightening on the lantern. "If Lena's anchor is here, how do we recognize it?"

Flicker flitted anxiously, its light dim. "It will resonate with her, something deeply tied to her past. A memory she couldn't let go of."

Mira's gaze swept across the scattered remnants—a silver locket swinging from an unseen breeze, a violin with snapped strings, an old book missing half its pages. Then she spotted it—a small, worn scarf draped over a broken fence post. The fabric was pale blue, embroidered with tiny stars.

Elias sucked in a sharp breath. "That's hers. I remember… she always wore that when we were kids. She said the stars would guide her home."

Mira reached for it, but the moment her fingers brushed the fabric, the mist around them surged violently. A deep tremor rolled through the Veil, and a low whispering chant filled the air.

"She is ours now... she belongs to the mist..."

The shadows deepened, coalescing into long, wraith-like figures. Their forms flickered between presence and absence, as though they were barely tethered to reality. Their hollow eyes fixed on Elias.

"You cannot take her back," one of the figures murmured. "She has been forgotten."

Elias stepped forward, defiance burning in his eyes. "She was never forgotten. I've been searching for her this whole time. I remember her. And that means she's still real."

The lantern in his hands flared, its golden light pushing back against the advancing darkness. The wraiths recoiled, their forms unraveling slightly.

Mira didn't hesitate. She grabbed the scarf and thrust it toward Elias. "If this is her anchor, then she needs to see it. She needs to remember."

The mist shuddered, and suddenly, a figure stepped into the flickering light—a girl with wide, disoriented eyes. Lena.

Elias took a shaky breath. "Lena, it's me. Come back."

For a moment, she hesitated, her form still wavering between the Veil and reality. Then, her gaze fell on the scarf, and recognition sparked in her eyes. Tears welled up as she whispered, "Elias?"

The lantern's light grew even brighter, and the wraiths let out a terrible, hollow wail. The Veil trembled, its grasp weakening.

Flicker darted forward. "Now! Call her name!"

Elias reached out, his voice ringing through the mist. "Lena! Come home!"

The world seemed to hold its breath.

Then, with a final surge of light, the Veil shattered around them.

A force like a great wind rushed past them, carrying whispers of memories as it fled into the darkness. The wraiths let out an unearthly shriek, dissolving into nothingness as the fabric of the Veil unraveled. Light poured in, golden and warm, illuminating the space that had once been consumed by shadows.

Lena collapsed to her knees, gasping for breath as if she had surfaced from drowning. Elias was beside her in an instant, his arms wrapping around her. "You're safe now."

She clung to him, her body trembling. "I thought I was lost forever. I tried to remember, but it kept pulling me deeper..."

Mira knelt beside them, offering a gentle smile. "You weren't forgotten. And now, you never will be."

Flicker hovered above them, its glow regaining its steady brilliance. "We must leave now. The Veil may be weakened, but it still lingers. We don't belong here."

Elias helped Lena to her feet, his grip firm and steady. As they turned toward the path leading out, the remnants of the Veil seemed to part for them, as if it, too, acknowledged their triumph.

With one final look at the dissipating mist, they stepped forward—toward home, toward hope, and toward the future they had nearly lost.

Chapter 18: The Path of Echoes

The air around them shimmered with the remnants of the Veil's collapse, a haze of fading whispers and dissolving shadows. The path before them twisted unnaturally, an eerie reflection of Moonvale distorted by the echoes of forgotten dreams. Flicker flitted ahead cautiously, its light pulsing as if sensing unseen dangers still lurking in the mist.

Mira tightened her grip on the Dreamkeeper's Lantern. "We should hurry. The Veil may have weakened, but we're not out yet."

Lena, still unsteady, clutched the star-embroidered scarf tightly in her hands. "It's strange... I feel like I've been here forever, yet I barely remember anything. It's like waking up from a dream you can't quite hold on to."

Elias cast a wary glance at their surroundings. "We'll get you home. Just stay close."

As they pressed forward, the landscape around them wavered. Fragments of memory flickered like mirages—glimpses of Moonvale as it once was, overlaid with the ghostly remnants of lost moments. Mira saw images of people moving about their daily lives, their faces blurred, their voices distant murmurs in the wind. Some smiled, some wept, others simply faded into the mist.

A soft rustling ahead made them all stop. The path ahead twisted and darkened, forming a corridor of shifting, spectral forms.

Flicker dimmed, hovering closer to Mira. "The Path of Echoes... It's where memories lost to the Veil linger. But be careful—some of them don't like to be remembered."

Before Mira could ask what that meant, the air turned icy, and the echoes solidified. Figures emerged from the mist—familiar yet wrong.

One of them stepped forward, its eyes hollow voids. "You don't belong here. Turn back."

Elias took a step forward, placing himself between the figure and Lena. "We're leaving. You can't stop us."

The echoes whispered in unison, their voices weaving together like a rising tide. "You took her from us. She was one of us now. She belongs here."

Lena gasped, gripping Elias's arm. "No. I don't. I remember who I am. I choose to leave."

The figures recoiled, their forms flickering as if Lena's words had wounded them. Mira raised the lantern, and the golden light radiated outward, pushing the shadows back. The Path of Echoes trembled, the illusion beginning to fracture.

"Keep moving!" Mira urged, leading the way as the echoes clawed at the edges of the fading Veil.

One last figure, barely more than a whisper of darkness, lingered as they passed. "Not all who leave truly return..." it murmured before vanishing into the mist.

With a final surge of determination, they stepped through the threshold—and into the waiting arms of dawn.

Chapter 19: The Rift's Closing

The dawn stretched across the sky, a delicate wash of pinks and golds, yet the path ahead still bore the lingering chill of the Veil. Mira, Elias, and Lena emerged from the mist, their steps heavy with exhaustion but steady with resolve. Flicker hovered close, its glow flickering like a candle caught in the wind.

Lena clutched her scarf tightly, her eyes darting toward the retreating mist. "It feels like... something's still watching us."

Elias tensed, glancing over his shoulder. "Maybe the Veil doesn't let go that easily."

Mira raised the lantern, and its golden light pulsed outward, dispelling the last tendrils of shadow. "We have to keep going. We're almost home."

As they stepped forward, the ground beneath them trembled. A low, guttural sound rumbled through the air—a final cry from the Veil. The path behind them convulsed, cracks spiderwebbing across its surface. The rift that had once bound Lena to the forgotten realm was closing.

"Run!" Flicker chirped, its wings a frantic blur.

Without hesitation, they sprinted forward, the ground beneath them shifting as the world behind them began to collapse. The Veil howled in protest, ghostly figures clawing at the edges of their retreat, their whispers desperate, longing.

"Lena—don't forget us!"

She faltered for the briefest moment, her breath hitching. The voices... they weren't angry. They were pleading. A strange ache settled in her chest—a part of her that had belonged to the Veil, a piece of herself that had once accepted the stillness of that place.

But Elias grabbed her hand, pulling her forward. "You belong with us. Keep going!"

The light ahead grew brighter as they neared the familiar outskirts of Moonvale. The weight of the Veil lessened with each step, the oppressive darkness retreating behind them. The moment their feet touched solid ground beyond the mist, the rift let out a final, thunderous crack—and then silence.

They turned back just in time to see the last remnants of the Veil fold in on itself and vanish, as if it had never been there.

Mira's heart pounded in her chest. "It's over."

Elias exhaled sharply, his grip on Lena's hand loosening. "We made it."

Lena took a shaky breath, her fingers brushing against the lantern. "I... I never thought I'd see the sun again."

But as the first golden rays of morning bathed Moonvale, something felt... different. The town was the same, its rooftops dusted in dawn's glow, the cobbled streets silent in the early light. And yet, the air carried an unnatural stillness, as if the world was waiting.

A whisper curled through the breeze, so faint it could have been imagined: "Not all doors close forever."

Mira's grip on the lantern tightened. The Veil had collapsed. But had it truly disappeared?

Chapter 20: The Return to Moonvale

The golden light of dawn stretched over Moonvale, casting long shadows across the quiet village. The familiar sight of cobbled streets and ivy-clad cottages should have brought Mira relief, yet something about it felt... different. The journey through the Veil had changed them—whether Moonvale had changed too, or if it was just their perception, she wasn't sure.

The three of them stood at the village entrance, their clothes still damp with mist, their limbs aching from exhaustion. Flicker hovered beside Mira, its glow dim but steady.

Lena took a deep breath, her eyes scanning the village square. "It's real," she whispered. "I'm really here."

Elias gave her a reassuring nod. "You are."

The silence was unnerving. Moonvale should have been waking by now—shopkeepers setting up stalls, bakers carrying fresh loaves from their ovens, children chasing each other down the streets. But everything felt still, almost hesitant, as if the town itself was holding its breath.

Then, from the eastern road, came the first sign of life. A woman gasped, dropping the basket she had been carrying, apples rolling onto the cobblestone. Her eyes widened as she took in the sight of Lena, her lips parting in disbelief.

"It's her," she murmured. "She's returned!"

The words spread like wildfire. Doors creaked open. Heads peeked from windows. In moments, the village square filled with murmurs and cautious steps. Then came the rush—people surrounding them, voices rising in wonder and shock.

"She was lost to the mist!"

"But they said no one ever comes back…"

"How is this possible?"

Mira felt the weight of the lantern in her hands, the warmth of its light pulsing gently. This was the moment she had fought for—bringing Lena home. Yet, as she looked at the faces of the villagers, she couldn't shake the feeling that something had followed them back.

Mayor Oswin pushed through the crowd, his usually composed expression crumbling into raw emotion. "Lena…" His voice wavered. "We thought—"

"I know," Lena interrupted, her own voice thick with emotion. "I thought so too."

The mayor hesitated, as if afraid she might disappear again. Then, in one swift movement, he pulled her into a tight embrace. A wave of relief swept through the villagers, and soon, others followed—hugs, tears, murmured prayers of gratitude. The village had lost many to the mist before. But now, for the first time, someone had come back.

Mira met Elias's gaze. He gave her a small, knowing smile. They had done it. They had broken the cycle.

And yet, in the back of her mind, a whisper of doubt remained.

Lena shifted uncomfortably under all the attention. "I... I need to sit," she admitted, and the mayor quickly ushered them toward the town hall.

As they walked, Mira stole a glance at the sky. The sun had fully risen now, its warmth chasing away the chill. But for the briefest moment, she swore she saw something shimmer along the horizon—a ripple in the air, as if the Veil had left behind a scar.

She blinked, and it was gone.

But the unease lingered, settling deep in her bones.

Not all doors close forever.

Chapter 21: The Final Mystery

That night, Moonvale celebrated. Lanterns hung from doorways, laughter filled the air, and for the first time in years, a true sense of joy pulsed through the village. The return of Lena was nothing short of a miracle, and the people embraced it with feasts and stories, as though willing to banish all memory of the mist's cruel history.

Mira, however, couldn't shake the feeling that something was still unfinished.

She stood at the edge of the village, staring toward the hills where the Veil had once loomed. The land there seemed normal—too normal. The mist was gone, and yet, when she closed her eyes, she could still hear the whispers.

"You feel it too, don't you?" Elias's voice cut through the quiet. He had followed her, his arms crossed as he stared at the darkened horizon.

Mira nodded. "It doesn't feel… over."

Elias frowned. "I saw it close. We all did."

"Then why does it feel like it's still watching?"

A gust of wind stirred the grass around them. It carried the scent of old parchment and something faintly metallic, like the air before a storm.

Flicker, who had been resting on Mira's shoulder, lifted into the air, its glow pulsing erratically. It spun in slow circles, as if sensing something unseen. Then, without warning, it darted toward the hills.

"Flicker!" Mira called, running after it. Elias was quick at her side.

The firefly's light guided them to an old oak tree at the village's border. Its gnarled roots twisted into the earth like reaching fingers, and at its base, half-buried in the dirt, lay something Mira had never seen before: a book.

It was ancient, its leather cover worn with age, the edges of its pages darkened as if touched by shadow. But what made Mira's breath catch in her throat was the symbol etched into the cover—

The same symbol that had been on the door to the Library of Lost Dreams.

Elias hesitated before reaching down. "Should we—"

Before he could finish, the book trembled. The air around it shimmered, and a voice, distant yet familiar, echoed in the wind.

"Not all doors close forever."

The book's cover creaked open on its own, revealing pages filled with ink that shifted like liquid gold. The words rearranged themselves before their eyes, forming a single sentence:

The Veil never truly disappears—it only waits.

Then, something else happened.

The air grew deathly still. The sounds of the festival behind them dulled, as if the world itself was holding its breath. Flicker, who had been hovering above them, suddenly dimmed, its glow nearly extinguished.

Mira's breath caught in her throat. Her fingertips tingled, and as she looked down, a faint, glowing mark appeared on her palm—the same symbol from the book. It burned, not painfully, but as if something had awakened inside her.

"Mira," Elias whispered, his voice tight. "What's happening?"

Before she could answer, a gust of wind swept through the clearing—but it wasn't natural. It carried with it the faintest tendrils of mist, barely visible, curling around their feet before vanishing like a dying breath.

A whisper, too soft to understand, curled through Mira's mind. Not a threat. Not a warning. But something in between.

A promise.

Then, just as suddenly, the wind died. The mist was gone. Flicker flared back to life, its light steady once more, and the book snapped shut with a soft thud.

Elias exhaled sharply. "Tell me that was just my imagination."

Mira looked at her palm, then at the book, then at the hills beyond. She knew better.

The Rift had closed. The mist had vanished. Lena had returned.

But the story wasn't over.

Epilogue: The Light Beyond the Veil

The stars shone brighter over Moonvale than they ever had before. The once-muted village was alive with music and laughter, lanterns swaying in the breeze as the festival carried on into the night. Children danced in the square, their laughter spilling through the cobbled streets, and families gathered outside their homes, sharing stories of dreams that had finally returned.

Mira stood at the crest of a small hill, overlooking the town. From here, she could see the river glistening under the moonlight, the willow tree swaying gently, and the Library of Lost Dreams, its doors now open to all who wished to remember. Lena sat on a bench just outside, her eyes filled with wonder as she read a book aloud to a small group of villagers.

Elias joined Mira, hands in his pockets. "They don't know, do they?"

Mira exhaled slowly. "Not yet."

He glanced at the book in her hands—the same book they had found beneath the oak tree. The symbol on the cover still glowed faintly, though it had dimmed since that night. She hadn't dared to open it again. Not yet.

"The mist is gone," Elias said after a pause. "The Rift is sealed. We should be able to move on."

"And yet…" Mira traced her fingers over the mark on her palm—the one that hadn't faded, no matter how many times she had tried to wash it away. "Something's still waiting."

A gust of wind stirred the grass around them, carrying a familiar scent—the same one she had noticed the night they found the book. Old parchment and the faintest trace of something metallic.

Mira turned toward the horizon. Beyond the hills, beyond the Rift, beyond what anyone in Moonvale could see, something had shifted.

She didn't know when, or how, but she knew one thing for certain: their journey wasn't over.

Elias sighed. "Guess we won't be getting much rest, huh?"

Mira smiled, gripping the book tightly. "Not anytime soon."

Flicker pulsed softly, its light steady, as if waiting.

As if ready.

And somewhere, beyond the stars, a new light flickered into existence.

END